The
Skimming
Stone

A short story about courage

Dominic Wilcox

I had carried the
golden skimming stone
for so, so long.

Waiting for the perfect moment
to release it into the world.

After thirty four years,
two months and twenty two days ...

... I knew the moment
had arrived at last.

I stood facing the mirrored lake
and felt a calmness descend.

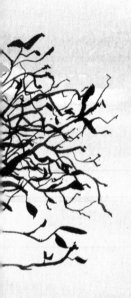

The stars had aligned.

It was the perfect balance
of stillness and silence.

I reached into my pocket
and took out the stone.

As I wrapped my finger
along its glimmering edge,
my mind started
to race with doubt.

'Will it skim and dance
on the surface,
the way it deserves
after all this time?'

'What if I throw it badly
and it just sinks slowly
into the depths?'

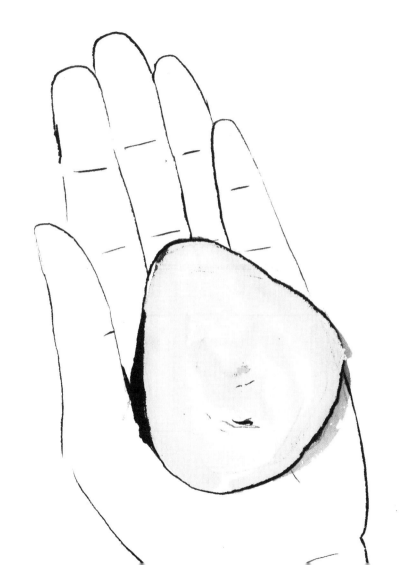

I looked at the stone
and it gleamed back at me
in such a beautiful way,
it was as though
it was speaking to me.

I felt calm again.

Stretched back my arm.

Took a deep breath.

And threw the golden stone
at the shimmering water's surface
with all my might.